JAZZ
AND BO'S
story

by
Sarah Hawkins

Illustrated by Artful Doodlers
Puzzle illustrations by Jason Chapman

RED FOX

BATTERSEA DOGS & CATS HOME: JAZZ AND BO'S STORY
A RED FOX BOOK 978 1 782 95180 3

First published in Great Britain by Red Fox,
an imprint of Random House Children's Publishers
A Random House Group Company

This edition published 2013

1 3 5 7 9 10 8 6 4 2

The Random House Group Limited supports the Forest Stewardship
Council® (FSC®), the leading international forest-certification organisation.
Our books carrying the FSC label are printed on FSC®-certified paper. FSC is
the only forest-certification scheme supported by the leading environmental
organisations, including Greenpeace. Our paper procurement policy can be
found at www.randomhouse.co.uk/environment.

MIX
Paper from
responsible sources
FSC® C016897

Set in 13/20 Stone Informal

Red Fox Books are published by Random House Children's Publishers,
61–63 Uxbridge Road, London W5 5SA

www.**randomhousechildrens**.co.uk
www.**randomhouse**.co.uk

Addresses for companies within The Random House Group Limited
can be found at: www.randomhouse.co.uk/offices.htm

THE RANDOM HOUSE GROUP Limited Reg. No. 954009

A CIP catalogue record for this book is available from the British Library.

Printed and bound in Great Britain by
CPI Group (UK) Ltd, Croydon, CR0 4YY

Turn to page 91 for lots
of information on
Battersea Dogs & Cats Home,
plus some cool activities!

Meet the stars of the Battersea Dogs & Cats Home series to date . . .

Bailey

Chester

Misty

Max

Daisy

Rusty

Snowy

Stella

Huey

Angel

Alfie

Cosmo

Buddy and Holly

Coco

Petal

Suzy

Bertie

Jessie

Oscar

Bruno

Sparkle and Belle

Buster

Pippin

Jazz and Bo

A Letter to Santa

"You're going to ruin Christmas, Harry!"
Abi shouted, as her brother ran out of the
room and slammed the door. Abi felt
tears come to her eyes. She'd been so
excited about putting the Christmas tree
up. Mum had got it out from the loft
while she and Harry were at school and
put it in the lounge, ready for them to
cover in tinsel and baubles. Abi's
favourite thing was putting the angel on

the top. But this year Harry didn't want to decorate it with her.

"Don't be a baby," Harry yelled back. Then Abi could hear him stomping up the stairs. Seconds later she heard the sound of him turning on his Xbox in his bedroom.

Abi stuck her tongue out at the door. *Stupid Harry*. He never wanted to do fun things with her anymore. Abi looked at the half-decorated Christmas tree and sighed. Christmas was her favourite time of year and Harry was spoiling everything!

"What are you two fighting about this time?" Mum said as she came into the lounge.

Abi pouted. "It's not me, it's Harry. I said I wanted to finish the tree and then watch a Christmassy film, but he said it was too babyish. Ever since you and Dad split up he's been mean, mean, mean."

"Oh honey," Mum gave her a squeeze. "I know it was hard for you two when Daddy and I got divorced, and last Christmas was a bit rotten, but this is where it all gets better. We're settled here now, and you're going

to have *two* Christmases – Christmas Eve
and Christmas Day with me and John,
then Boxing Day and the day after with
Daddy and Sandra! Won't that be good?"

Abi shrugged.

"Come on, we can finish this." Mum
said. "And you can put the angel on top,
even though it's Harry's turn."

That made Abi smile.

"There!" Mum said as they put on the last bauble. Then she put on a fake TV presenter voice and pretended to talk into a microphone. "And now, our special guest, turning on the Christmas lights – Abi Harper!"

Abi giggled as she went over to the plug socket and pushed the switch.

The Christmas tree sparkled with twinkly white lights, and suddenly everything seemed festive and exciting again. "Ahhhhh," she and Mum sighed.

Mum gave her a hug. "Now, have you written your letter to Santa yet?"

Abi shook her head. "Go on then," Mum said, shooing her upstairs. Abi ran up to her room, banging on her brother's door as she went past. "The tree looks BEAUTIFUL," she yelled through the door. "No thanks to you, Harry!"

Abi went to her desk and chose her best pen, the pink one with the fluffy bit on the top, and the special notepaper she'd got for her birthday. It had kittens all over it. Abi looked at their cute faces and had an idea. There was only one thing she really, really wanted — and maybe Santa would bring it for her! She sat down and started writing as neatly as she could:

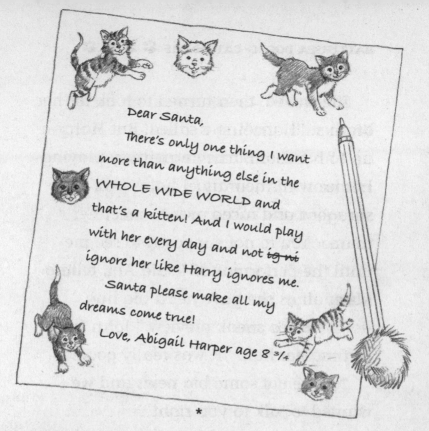

Dear Santa,
There's only one thing I want more than anything else in the WHOLE WIDE WORLD and that's a kitten! And I would play with her every day and not ~~ig ni~~ ignore her like Harry ignores me. Santa please make all my dreams come true!
Love, Abigail Harper age 8 ¾

*

"Beautiful!" Mrs Sharpe cried. "Well done, everyone, this is going to be the best carol concert ever!"

Abi grinned as she stepped down from the stage, being careful not to trip over her long, white angel costume. Just then she spotted her mum and John at the back of the hall.

She waved, then turned to look for her brother. "Harry!" she called. But Harry and his friend Barney were busy playing Frisbee with their angel halos. Abi shrugged and raced over to meet her mum. "You're not supposed to see me until the performance!" said Abi, telling Mum off as she gave her a big hug.

"We got a sneak preview," John said, ruffling her hair. "It was really good."

"We've got some big news and we wanted to talk to you right away," Mum explained.

"Harry!" John called. Harry waved goodbye to his friends and ran over, fiddling with the cotton wool of his shepherd beard.

"I'm afraid you're going to have to ask
Santa for something else, Abi," Mum
said. Abi's heart sank. *The kitten!* She'd
been so sure that Santa could get her one.

"What did you ask for?" Harry said,
curiously.

"A kitten," Abi replied sadly.

"And Santa can't give you a kitten,"
Mum continued, sounding serious,
"because that's what John and I are
getting for you!"

Abi gasped. Mum had a huge,
beaming smile on her face.
She squeezed Abi's hand
excitedly. Abi couldn't
believe it. She looked
from Mum to John,
who nodded too.
Then she flung
herself at Mum

and hugged her tightly round the waist.
"Eeeeeek!" she squealed excitedly.

"I've always wanted a cat," Mum said
excitedly.

Abi thought about having a tiny, fluffy
kitten of her very own
and jumped up and
down, her angel
wings flapping
against her back.
"This is the best
thing that's
happened to me in
my whole entire
life!"
Abi turned to her
brother, but to her
surprise, Harry's face looked grumpy. "No
fair," he grumbled, "If Abi gets a kitten,
then *I* want a puppy!"

Fighting Like Cats and Dogs

"For the last time, we can't get a kitten *and* a puppy, they'd fight more than you two do!" Mum said as they got on the train.

They were on their way to a place called Battersea Dogs' and Cats' Home, where kind people looked after animals until they found a family of their own. Abi looked down at her gloves, which

had smiling cat faces
on them, and
grinned.

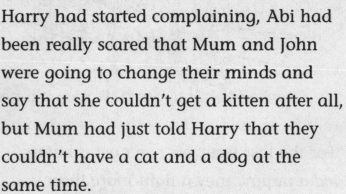

She still couldn't
believe she was
getting a kitten! When
Harry had started complaining, Abi had
been really scared that Mum and John
were going to change their minds and
say that she couldn't get a kitten after all,
but Mum had just told Harry that they
couldn't have a cat and a dog at the
same time.

"You only want a pet because I'm
getting one," Abi whispered to her big
brother. "I saw your letter to Santa and
you asked for Xbox games."

"I've ALWAYS wanted a dog," Harry
replied crossly. "I just didn't think I would
be allowed one." Abi knew it was true –

her brother did love dogs. On his old
Nintendo DS he'd had a game where he
had to look after a dog and feed it and
play with it. He'd even had dog gloves
like her cat ones until he said they were
too babyish. Still, she stuck her tongue
out at him.

"Maybe we can get a dog when the
kitten's a bit older," John said.

"Anyway, think about how nice it'll be
to have a little kitten in the house." Mum
told Harry. "I'm sure
Abi will let you
play with him or
her."

"You can't
take a kitten
for walks,"
Harry
grumbled.

It was already dark when they came
out of the train station. Christmas lights
twinkled in all the shop windows, and
there were pretty wreaths on the doors of
all the houses. Abi felt so happy that she
couldn't help skipping as she went along,
holding Mum and John's hands. Harry
walked next to them sulkily, scuffing his
shoes.

Finally they reached a huge set of
gates. Inside them was a big curved glass
building, and another tall building with
the Battersea Dogs' and Cats' Home logo

on it – a huge blue circle with a dog and
a cat curled up next to one another.

"See, dogs and cats *can* be friends,"
Harry muttered.

They went through the gate, past an
enormous Christmas tree, and into
Reception. As Mum explained to the
receptionist why they were there, Abi
looked around excitedly. There was
a little shop that sold all kinds of
cat and dog things – even
stockings for cats and
dogs to put up
for Santa!

She and mum had already been
shopping and bought everything a kitten
would need. Abi had picked out a cosy
cat bed, a pink food and water bowl with
fishes painted on it and a covered litter
tray that would be the kitten's very own
bathroom. Abi felt bad as she saw Harry
looking longingly at the dog leads.

She snuck over to him.
"What colour cat do
you think we should
get?" she asked
him, trying to be
friendly.

Harry shrugged,
but he didn't look
quite as cross as before.

"Abi! Harry!" Mum
called them over to meet a smiling lady.

"I'm Lauren," she said with a big grin.

"I hear you're looking for a kitten," she said to Abi.

Abi nodded excitedly. Lauren led them next door to the glass building, talking as she went. "Well, we've got lots of cats, but there aren't really many kittens at Christmas time," she explained. "Most of them are born in the summer. But we do have one in at the moment. Sadly her owners had to move abroad and they couldn't take their pets with them. Would you like to see her?"

Abi suddenly felt really nervous. *If there was only one kitten, what if it wasn't the right one?*

Her tummy felt swirly and shaky as Lauren led her over to a spiral staircase, with Mum, John and Harry behind her.

The stairs led up into the middle of a
room. All around the edges were pens
with glass doors, and inside each one was
a different cat!

Some were staring
though the door, or
playing with toys,
but most of them
were curled up on
the beds. "They've
got heated pads in their
baskets," Lauren told her, "so they're
really cosy and warm,
no matter how
cold and
miserable it is
outside!"

Lauren led
them over to a little

room full of cat toys. There were toy mice
and balls and some fishing rods with
dangly bright things on the end. In the
corner of the room there was a huge
scratching post that was as big as Abi,
with lots of flat levels for the cats to climb
on.

"I'll bring Jazz in here so you can meet
her properly," Lauren said.

Jazz thought Abi as Lauren left. *Was that the kitten's name?* It was such a pretty one, and so fun too! The door creaked open. Abi held her breath. *What would Jazz be like?*

Lauren came back in holding a small, fluffy, completely adorable, black-and-white kitten! She had a white stripe down her nose and bright blue eyes. When Abi looked at Jazz all her worries disappeared. She was absolutely perfect!

Jazz and Bo

Lauren carefully shut the door and put Jazz down. There was a flash of black-and-white, and the little kitten ran and hid under the sofa where Mum and John were sitting!

They jumped up in surprise. "She's OK!" Lauren laughed, "cats often hide when they're a bit nervous."

Abi crouched down and peered underneath the sofa. Jazz stared back at her, her blue eyes wide. "It's OK, Jazz," Abi called. "We won't hurt you."

As Abi looked at the kitten's twitching ears, she had an idea. She jumped up and got one of the cat toys, one with a pink feather that dangled on the end of a string. She poked the feather under the sofa and wiggled it about. Suddenly, Jazz put out at paw and batted it. Abi giggled. She put the feather back under, then slowly dragged it out. Jazz rushed out from under the sofa to catch it.

Abi gently reached out to stroke Jazz's black-and-white fur. She was so soft and very fluffy! Abi stroked Jazz's head and the kitten wriggled round happily. As she clawed at the feather, Abi saw the little pink pads on the underside of her tiny paws. She was the cutest thing Abi had ever seen!

"Awww!" Mum squealed as Abi and
Jazz played. Even Harry laughed when
Jazz stood up on her back legs, reaching
up to catch the feather.

"She got over her
shyness quickly,
didn't she?"
Mum said to
Lauren.

"She likes having someone to play with." Lauren nodded. "I think she just misses her sister."

"Where is she?" Abi asked.

Lauren chuckled. "Well, they're not *really* sisters, they just grew up together. Bo is in the dogs' home."

Abi gasped.

Harry's eyes lit up. "She's a dog?"

"I thought dogs and cats didn't like each other?" Mum asked.

"It really depends on the animals," Lauren explained. "If you already have a dog or cat and you get a new pet they might fight, and some cats are scared of dogs – and some dogs are scared of cats.

Every animal is different. These two have
been together ever since they were babies,
and they really think they're sisters. We'd
have liked to have homed them together,
but not many people have time or room
for a new dog *and* cat."

Harry looked at Abi, and she knew just
what he was thinking. Abi glanced from
the gorgeous kitten to her brother's happy
face and grinned.

"We do!" they said together.

*

"Let's go and see this dog first, before you get all excited," Mum said. Minutes later, it was all arranged. Lauren put Jazz in a comfy cat carrier, and they traipsed next door to the dogs' home.

Abi peered anxiously inside the basket as Mum carried it along, but Jazz was curled at the back cosily. "We're going to see your sister!" Abi told her.

Harry was walking so fast that the others had to half-run to catch up. "Just wait until I tell Dad!" Harry said excitedly.

The dogs' home was completely different from the cats' home. Lauren led them down a slope to a room with pens on either side. "Bo should be somewhere around . . . here!" she said, pointing to one of the pens. Inside, a little brown puppy was sitting sadly in her basket.

"A boxer!" Harry said excitedly when he saw her.

"That's right!" Lauren told him. "She's about nine weeks old, the same as Jazz."

"Bo!" Harry called, bending down and putting his hand out. Bo jumped up, her tail wagging. She had a gorgeous wrinkly face, and she was a golden brown colour all over, apart from a white stripe down her nose and on her paws.

Bo raced over to the door and stood up on her hind legs, straining to sniff at Harry's hand.

"I must smell like Jazz!" Harry laughed as the puppy snuffled at his fingers. Lauren opened the pen door, and Harry and Abi both bent down to stroke Bo as she rushed out, her tail wagging excitedly. Abi stroked

Bo's short brown fur and the puppy wriggled happily. She was so different from Jazz, but just as cute!

Then Bo raced over to Mum and jumped up at the cat basket, sniffing excitedly.

"*Woof!*" she barked.

From inside the basket came a tiny answering "*miaow!*"

Bo's tail wagged happily.

"Yes, it's your sister!" Lauren laughed. "Do you want to go and see her? Let's take her into one of the dog meeting rooms, then we can let Jazz out."

Harry held Bo's lead as they walked to the meeting room. Abi could see her brother bursting with pride as he walked with the little puppy trotting next to him.

"Here we are," Lauren said, leading them into the meeting room which had a table and chairs, a dog basket and some doggy toys, as well as a window looking down onto the courtyard, where the lights on the Christmas tree were twinkling.

"Ready to let Jazz out?" Lauren asked.

Abi nodded. She couldn't wait to see what happened when the little cat and dog saw each other! Mum put the cat

basket down on the table, and Abi
opened the little door.

Jazz padded out onto the table
nervously, but when she saw Bo she sat
up and gave a loud *"miaow"*.

"Woof!" Bo replied happily, standing
up on her back legs and straining to
reach Jazz. *"Woof, woof, woof!"*

"Oh, she's gorgeous!" Mum cried.
"She's such a cuddly little puppy!"

Jazz leaped down from the table to
the chair, and Bo rushed to meet her.
Jazz jumped down and
raced straight
between Bo's
front paws,
nudging her
head up
against Bo's
chin.

"They love each other!" Abi gasped.

Jazz started purring loudly as Bo gave her ear a friendly lick.

Abi knelt down in front of them and stroked Jazz's back. She was so happy she couldn't stop smiling. "Don't you think it's perfect, Mum?" she asked. "A cat for me and a dog for Harry!" She turned to Mum, but to her surprise, Mum was looking at John worriedly.

"I don't know, Abi," Mum shook her head. "A new dog *and* a new cat is a lot of work, and we'd have to look after them when you have your weekends with your dad . . ."

Abi stared at Harry, who looked as
dismayed as she felt.

"You don't have to decide right away,"
Lauren said, looking at Mum and John.
"You can think about it."

Lauren took Bo outside. As she shut
the door, Jazz tried to follow, and Abi had
to hold her. As soon as the
door closed they heard a
mournful howl from
outside. Jazz raced over to
the door and put her front
paws up at it. As Bo gave
another howl she gave a
long crying "*miaow*", then
another, and another.

"What do you need to
think about?" Harry said
fiercely. "Bo and Jazz *need*
us, and it's *Christmas*."

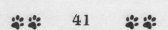

"Please, Mum," Abi picked up Jazz.
The little kitten snuggled into her arms
but she didn't take her eyes off the door.
Then she looked up at Abi and gave a
sad, confused little *"miaow"*. She didn't
understand why her sister had gone
away. Abi understood – she'd felt sad and
confused too when her parents had split
up. "It'll be OK, Jazz," Abi said. "I
promise."

Abi looked out of the window, but it
was so dark all she could
see was the reflection
of herself, holding
the fluffy baby
kitten. Abi
hugged Jazz close
and made up her
mind. "I don't
want to take Jazz

away from her sister. If we can't have Bo too, then we should let Jazz stay here and wait for someone that can have them both."

"Are you sure?" Mum said.

Abi nodded, not trusting herself to speak. It would break her heart to leave Jazz behind, but she couldn't take her away from Bo.

"OK, well—" Mum started.

"You know," John interrupted. "I had dogs all the time when I was growing up. Harry and Abi are both old enough to be responsible. You'd feed Bo and walk her, wouldn't you, Harry?"

Abi felt a glimmer of hope. She turned to look at John and Mum.

Harry nodded fiercely. "I'd even pay for her food. I'll . . . I'll sell my Xbox."

John grinned. "There's no need for that, but you do have to promise to help out every single day."

"I will." Harry promised.

"Me too," Abi agreed.

"I think we should get them both. Besides," John added, "a dog and a cat can't be more trouble than these two!"

Mum looked from Harry to Abi and her face broke into a smile. "I suppose it *would* be the best Christmas present ever . . ."

"Yes!" Harry jumped up and punched the air. "Thanks Mum!" he yelled, giving her a huge hug. Then he threw his arms around John as well. John looked a bit surprised, then patted Harry on the back.

Abi hugged Jazz, and the kitten looked up at her. "We're getting Bo too," Abi said, kissing her fluffy head. "You're going to be with your sister!" Jazz started making a lovely deep purring sound.

"Quick, let's get Bo back!" Harry cried. He flung open the door. Lauren was stood outside, holding the puppy with a huge smile on her face. "I was so hoping that you'd be the right family for them!" she grinned. "Bo and Jazz belong together!"

Christmas Carols

"You'll never guess!" Abi said. She smiled as she heard her dad's deep chuckle down the phone.

"Go on then, tell me," he laughed.

"A kitten!" Abi shrieked. "And Harry's getting a puppy!"

"A kitten *and* a puppy!" Dad exclaimed. "Mum's house is going to be full of animals!"

"Isn't that brilliant?" Abi said, picking

up a present from under the tree and
shaking it.

"Very brilliant," Dad
replied.

"Oh and I've got
more news!" Abi told
him as she carefully
put the present back.

"What else? Dad joked.
"Are you getting an elephant as well?"

Abi giggled. "No silly, can you come to
my carol concert? It's on the 20th
December at 7pm. We get to go to school
when it's all dark!"

"On the 20th? Hmm, I don't know."
Dad hesitated. "I'd love to hear you sing,
darling, but it's not my night to see you . . .
I know, you can give me and Sandra an
extra-special performance when you come
round."

"OK," Abi said sadly. The bang of a car door made her jump, and she looked up to see a lady in a familiar blue jumper coming down the drive. She was wearing a Christmas hat and she had a piece of purple tinsel round her neck like a scarf.

"Dad – I've got to go, the lady from Battersea is here!" she squealed.

It was two weeks after they'd met Bo and Jazz. Mum and John had done all the paperwork, and the only thing left to do was for someone from Battersea to come round and check that their house would make a good home for two special new pets!

Abi and Harry had tidied their rooms
specially, and Mum had taken Harry
back to the Battersea shop to buy doggy
versions of all the things they'd already
got for Jazz. Now Bo's doggy
basket was sitting
proudly in the
lounge next to
Jazz's. Bo's basket
was twice as
large as Jazz's
though – she and
Jazz were almost
the same size now, but
Bo would grow a *lot* bigger.

"Mum! John! Harry!" Abi called as she
ran to open the front door. The lady from
Battersea rushed inside, blowing on her
hands to warm them up. "Merry
Christmas!" she grinned, "I'm Edna."

They showed Edna all round the house and garden, then Mum took everyone into the kitchen for some hot chocolate.

Abi put marshmallows on the top of her drink and nervously watched as they melted.

"Everything looks fine!" Edna said, and Abi blew out a big breath. "Bo and Jazz are very lucky to have found you." She smiled. "But there are going to be a few challenges to having a dog and a cat. Even though they're both coming home at the same time, they have very different needs. Bo will have to be walked every day, whereas Jazz will be able to go in and out of the cat flap."

"John just put a cat flap in the back door," Abi showed her.

Edna nodded. "But Jazz will have to be kept inside for two weeks until she gets used to her new home. Otherwise she might get confused about which house is hers and not be able to find her way back. I think they're going to be very happy here." Edna took a slurp of hot chocolate. "Bo and Jazz are yours whenever you'd like to pick them up!"

That night Abi dreamed about Santa coming in the cat flap to leave presents for Jazz and Bo. She couldn't wait for her kitten to arrive!

Welcome Home!

"We're home!" John called as he opened the front door and Bo bounded inside. He put down the cat carrier and brushed the snow off Bo's coat. "And it's snowing!" he exclaimed, as he shut the door.

Abi ran down the stairs two at a time, followed by Mum and Harry.

"Hello Bo!" Abi called. The puppy ran over and jumped at her legs happily. Harry rushed over to greet the little

puppy, and soon they were rolling about
on the floor together. Abi excitedly
opened the door of the cat carrier. Mum,
John and Harry all watched excitedly as
she opened the door
wide, but no kitten
appeared.
"Welcome home,
Jazz!" Abi
squealed,
kneeling down
and peering into
the basket. Jazz was
right at the back of the carrier, crouched
down nervously, just like she had under
the sofa.

"It's ok," Abi said, reaching in to
stroke her. Jazz gave a purr and snuggled
into Abi's hand, but she didn't move from
the cat carrier. Bo scrambled over to the

basket and gave a delighted *"woof!"*
There was a tiny *"mew"* from inside the
basket. Bo barked again, her tail wagging
happily, and Jazz replied, meowing
louder this time.

"She'll come out in her own time,"
Mum said. But Bo couldn't wait.

"Woof, woof!" The little puppy barked
happily, then rushed forwards and tried
to get inside the cat
carrier with Jazz!
Abi caught the
wriggly puppy
just as his bum
disappeared into
the cat box.
"Soon she'll be
too big to do that," John laughed.

But seeing her sister seemed to have
done the trick. When Abi pulled Bo out,

Jazz came out after her,
stepping onto the
carpet delicately.

"*Woof! Woof!*"
Bo barked
happily,
crouching with her
bum in the air so
that she was the same
height as Jazz. She dashed
round in a circle, her tail wagging so
hard that it hit the lower branches of the
Christmas tree.

"Come on Bo," Harry called. "I'll show
you all your things."

Bo galloped after Harry. Jazz gave a
little "*meow*" as her sister disappeared,
and she trotted after them. Abi giggled as
Harry led the dog and the cat into the
kitchen.

Jazz went into her covered litter tray
and soon they could hear the sound of
her paws crunching on the gravelly
catlitter. Bo went to investigate the noise.

"Let's take Bo outside in case she needs
the loo too," Mum suggested.

While Harry opened the back door,
Abi rolled a jingly ball along the floor to
distract Jazz. Jazz watched it with her ears
pricked up, then scampered after it and
pounced on it.

Harry and Bo came back inside. "It's still snowing!" Harry grinned. Bo ran into the middle of the kitchen and shook herself so that droplets of snow spattered everywhere.

"Bo!" Mum laughed.

Bo flopped down and gave a big puppy yawn.

"I think they're tired after their long day," Mum said. "Shall we watch a Christmassy film, the whole family together?"

"Yes!" Abi replied.

"As long as Bo can sit with me!" Harry grinned as they rushed into the lounge, the kitten and puppy chasing at their feet.

"No animals on the sofa," Mum called.

"They can't sit on the sofa with us," Harry whispered to Abi. "But she didn't say we couldn't sit on the floor with them!"

While Harry went to find the film, and Mum went to make them some popcorn, Abi made a nest of cushions on the floor, leaning against the sofa. She put Bo and Jazz's new beds next to her, but Jazz snuggled into her lap instead.

Abi looked at her two new family members and gave a huge smile. She couldn't believe they were really

here – and they were hers and Harry's forever!

Just then there was a funny noise. Abi looked up and gasped. "Bo's eating the Christmas tree!" she yelled as the puppy streaked by with a long line of tinsel in her mouth. Jazz leaped off Abi's lap and pounced at the tinsel as Bo dragged it past her.

Abi laughed delightedly as she untangled the naughty animals and took the tinsel out of Bo's mouth.

Things were going to be so much fun now Bo and Jazz were here!

A Brilliant Idea?

"While shepherds washed their *socks* at night . . ." Harry sang loudly.

"MUM!" Abi yelled. "He's doing it again!"

"Stop being a baby," Harry told her.

"We need to practise *properly*," she told him importantly. "The carol concert is tomorrow."

Abi was sitting at the piano in her angel costume. She'd wanted Harry to

wear his shepherd's costume too, but he'd
only put the beard on. He was standing
next to her with Bo sitting at his feet, and
Jazz was curled up on her favourite place
– Abi's lap.

"Come on, try it
again," Mum
called from the
kitchen. "It
sounds lovely."

"Sounds
better with my
words," Harry
grumbled.

"Sing it properly,
Harry," Abi said bossily, putting her
fingers on the keys. "And turn the page
or I'll do it wrong."

"While shepherds *watched their flocks*
by night," she started. This time Harry

sang all the right words. Abi quickly turned the book to the next carol and started to play it. "Ding dong merrily on high!" she and Harry sang. But just as they were getting to the chorus, another voice joined in. "*Woof! Woof!*" Bo barked.

Harry and Abi dissolved into giggles. Jazz looked up in interest as Abi's laughter jiggled her around.

Harry reached down to pet Bo, whose plump little tail wagged happily. "Good girl, Bo," he laughed.

They started again. "Ding dong—" but Bo joined in again – and every time she barked, Jazz miaowed in reply!

"Gloo-ooo-orrrrr-RIA!" Harry and Abi sang, and Bo gave a long howl.

"*Miaow!*" Jazz added, padding up to Bo and nudging her head against the puppy's chin. Bo reached down and gave her a friendly lick.

"Awww!" Abi grinned. She didn't mind Jazz and Bo singing along, they were so cute!

"I hope Bo doesn't do that at the actual concert," Mum laughed, coming in to the lounge and wiping her hands on a tea towel.

"Is she coming?" Abi asked.

"Yes," Mum said. "She needs a walk anyway, and this way she gets to see you two too!"

"But what about Jazz?" Abi asked.

"Ha, ha, that's why dogs are so much better than cats," Harry teased. "You can take them places and do things with them."

"Whatever, Harry," Abi scooped up Jazz and took her upstairs to her bedroom. She put Jazz down carefully on the bed, then flomped down next to her. Jazz walked over and sniffed her, then climbed up on Abi's tummy and curled up, purring loudly.

Abi stroked her warm, soft body and Jazz nuzzled into her hand. Then, with a funny chirping sound like a bird, Jazz rolled over and stretched out for a tummy tickle.

"I love you so much, Jazz," Abi said, "and it's so not fair that you won't be there at the carol concert when Bo gets to come."

Abi felt Jazz's little paws. "You don't want to stay here all on your own, do you?" Jazz stared up at her, her blue eyes wide. Abi stroked her head and tickled her ears and Jazz started purring.

Abi hugged the little kitten closely. She had a brilliant idea!

A Special Performance

"Oh Abi, you look beautiful, like a real angel!" Grandma said, giving Abi a huge hug. It was the night of the carol concert, and Grandma and Grandpa had come to meet Bo and Jazz before they all went to watch Harry and Abi perform.

"And Jazz is just the most gorgeous little kitten," she added, stroking her between the ears.

Bo was jumping around everyone's

legs, excited to see so many people, and Jazz trotted after her sister wherever she went.

"Now, let's go and put Jazz safely upstairs," Mum said. After researching how to make Jazz feel safe in the house by herself, they'd decided to keep her in Abi's room for the evening, where she'd be nice and snuggly, and couldn't escape. Abi had already moved Jazz's litter box and her feed bowls up there, and made sure there was nothing the little kitten could hurt herself on. "She'll probably sleep the whole evening and not even know that we're gone." Mum had said cheerfully.

"I'll do it," Abi said quickly. She picked Jazz up, and took her up to her room. A few minutes later Abi came back down with her school bag in her arms. "Bye, Jazz!" she called up the stairs. "We'll be home soon."

"Good girl," Mum said. "Now, everyone in the car!" If we don't go soon, Christmas will be over before we get there!"

*

When they got to school, all the grown-
ups went to sit in the audience and Harry
and Abi went to find their classmates. As
soon as she got to the back of the hall,
Abi checked no one was watching, then
rushed out into the school corridor and
snuck over to her classroom. She crept
inside and carefully shut the door. The
room looked different in the dark, and it
was a bit scary until Abi
turned on the lights to
see the paper
snowflake decorations
on all the walls. She
looked around for the
best place, then
carefully put her school
bag down in the library corner. It was a
cosy spot with lots of cushions and books.

Double-checking the door was shut,
Abi carefully opened her bag – and let
Jazz out!

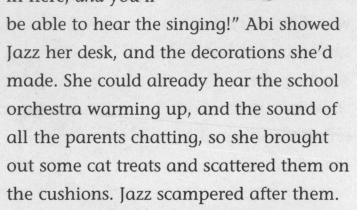

"There!" Abi said
happily as Jazz
settled down on
the cushions.
"You'll be nice
and cosy and safe
in here, *and* you'll
be able to hear the singing!" Abi showed
Jazz her desk, and the decorations she'd
made. She could already hear the school
orchestra warming up, and the sound of
all the parents chatting, so she brought
out some cat treats and scattered them on
the cushions. Jazz scampered after them.

"See you after the show, Jazz!" Abi
grinned. Jazz purred happily as she
gobbled up the treats.

Abi raced into the hall and up onto
the stage just as the first song was
starting. Harry gave her a curious look,
but she just smiled. Out in the audience
she could see Mum, John, Grandma and
Grandpa. Mum was sniffing and wiping
her eyes as she grinned. Bo was perched
on her lap, sitting and watching happily,
her tongue poking out as she gave a
doggy smile. Grandma and Grandpa
waved, and John was bobbing his
head to the music with a
big smile on his face.

Then
someone
else

caught Abi's eye, and she saw Dad and
Sandra sitting at the other
side of the hall. Dad
waved and blew kisses.
Abi gasped in surprise,
then had to
concentrate on her
words. It was hard to
sing, she was smiling so
much. Everyone she loved
was here – even Jazz!

All too soon, the show was finished.
The audience cheered and clapped, and
Abi could hear Bo barking as well as
Mum shouting, "More! More!"

She glanced at Harry and he grinned
at her. Then Mrs Allerton nodded at her
and she stepped forward. Mum and John
had come to the rehearsal, but they
hadn't seen this bit. Abi took at deep

breath and thought about Jazz in the
next room. Then she started her solo,
singing loudly and clearly so the little
kitten would hear her. "Oh, little town of
Bethlehem . . ." she sang. When she
finished the verse, the choir joined in and
they sang the rest of the song together.
Abi felt like she was going to burst with
pride.

As soon as the
concert was over,
Mum ran up to Abi
and picked her up,
swinging her
round in an
enormous hug. "You
were so brilliant!" she
shrieked. "And a solo! That
was the best Christmas surprise ever!"

"Well done, Abs," Harry said. John
handed him Bo's lead and the puppy
danced around his feet, barking excitedly.

"Well done, darling!" Dad swept her
up in a huge hug and patted Harry on
the back. "You were both brilliant!"

"Dad, how come you're here?" Abi
said delightedly.

"Mum and I sorted it out," Dad said.
"Isn't that good?"

"Brilliant!" Abi was smiling so much her face ached.

"Go and get your things and then we'll go home and celebrate," Mum told them.

Abi nodded – she couldn't wait to see Jazz!

She followed all the other angels as they went laughing and joking to pick up their bags, but when they got to the back of the hall Abi slipped away. But as she got close to her classroom she saw something that made her tummy jump in fear – the door was open.

"Jazz?" Abi whispered. But there was no sign of the kitten anywhere.

Fighting back tears, Abi ran back into the hall. Harry was standing in the middle of his school friends, who were fussing and petting Bo. Abi grabbed her brother and whispered to him. "Harry, something horrible's happened." She sobbed. "I brought Jazz to the carol concert, and now she's gone!"

Christmas Crisis!

"I just wanted her to hear my solo, and Bo was coming," Abi tried to explain. She felt shaky and sick. Harry looked very cross.

"Abi, you know that Jazz is meant to stay at home," he said. "She's a cat, not a dog."

"I know!" Abi said, tears spilling out of her eyes and dripping off her nose. "Please help me find her."

"OK," Harry said, giving her a quick hug. "We'll find her. But we've got to tell Mum and John."

"They'll be so cross!" Abi sobbed.

"But we've got to find her, and they can help us look." Harry said.

Abi thought about Jazz in the school somewhere, lost and alone, and nodded.

"You take Bo and go and look in the classroom," Harry told her. "I'll get Mum."

Abi nodded. She was so scared she couldn't speak. She grabbed Bo's lead. The little puppy looked up at her and whined. "We've got to find Jazz," she whispered, a huge lump in her throat.

"She's lost and it's all my fault!"

Bo looked up at her as if she understood every word. *"Woof!"* she agreed.

Abi ran back to the classroom as fast as she could, with Bo running alongside her. They burst into the quiet room.

"Jazz!" Abi called again. "Jazz!" She started looking under the desks, thinking about when Jazz had hidden before.

"Woof! Woof!" Bo called.

But there was no sign of the kitten anywhere.

"Oh Bo, what am I
going to do?" Abi said,
picking up the puppy
and hugging her
tightly. "I need to find
Jazz!" *If she wasn't in
the classroom, where
was she?* Abi started
crying as she thought
about the tiny kitten lost
in the huge school.

Bo wriggled to be put down.
"*Woof!*" she barked again. "*Woof, woof,
woof, woof!*"

Abi bent to put her down – but as she
did she heard a noise – an answering
"*miaow!*"

"Bo! Bark again!" Abi said excitedly.
Just then she had an idea. She took
a deep breath and started to sing.

"Gloo-oor-ooo-ooria". Bo looked up at her, her plump tail wagging.

"Come on Bo," Abi sniffed. "Gloooooooo-oooria!"

Bo gave a big doggy grin and opened her mouth. *"Woof, Wooowooooowf!"* she howled.

Abi strained her ears, listening for the tiniest sound. Suddenly she heard something! A little *"miaow!"* joining in. It was coming from the library corner!

Abi raced over to the corner and flung the cushions aside. There, blinking up at her sleepily, was Jazz!

"OH, Jazz!" Abi picked her up and gave her a huge hug.

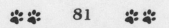

As she hugged her happily, Mum,
John and Harry rushed into the room,
followed by Grandma and Grandpa.
"We'll split up and search the whole
school," Mum said.

"It's OK," Abi sniffed.
"Bo found her."

"Oh thank
goodness! Well
done, Bo!" Mum
said. Harry went
to give his
puppy a hug.
John and
Grandpa
gathered round
Harry and praised
Bo, while Mum and
Grandma went to comfort
Abi and fuss over Jazz.

Mum bent down
and looked at Abi
seriously. "Abigail,
you did a VERY
silly thing. Jazz
could have been
seriously hurt. You
know that don't you?"

Abi nodded. "I thought
I'd lost her," she whispered.

"You were very lucky you didn't."
Mum said. "I told you that looking after
pets was a responsibility, and you weren't
very responsible AT ALL. You're not
getting any more pocket money until the
end of January, and I expect you to give
Jazz her breakfast every morning without
being asked. OK? And I wouldn't be
surprised if Santa puts you on his
naughty list rather than his nice list."

Abi nodded again. "I'm really sorry, Mum," she said. "I'll never do anything like that EVER again."

"OK." Mum opened her arms and gave her and Jazz a big hug. "Jazz's OK and that's the most important thing." She stroked Jazz and she purred contentedly.

"Did you find her?" Dad asked as he and Sandra burst into the room. "Oh thank goodness," he sighed as he saw the little kitten in Abi's arms.

"Jazz, this is Dad, and Sandra." Abi introduced them. Dad bent down and tickled Jazz behind the ears. "She's beautiful," he said. Then he kissed Abi on the top of her head.

Sandra gave Abi a huge hug. "We haven't decorated the Christmas tree yet," she said. "We've been waiting for you to come round."

"Let's go home," Mum said. "You've had quite enough adventures for one night, Jazz."

"Can we do some more carols?" Harry asked.

"Oh yes," said Grandma, "I want to hear Abi's solo again."

"If we do some singing at home Bo and Jazz might join in!" Abi grinned, and started telling Dad all about their funny carol practice and how that had helped her find Jazz.

"We can do more carols, and I've got mulled wine and hot chocolate at home," Mum told them. "And mince pies."

"Just keep hold of Jazz," John told Abi. "We don't want to lose her again." Abi rubbed her cheek against Jazz's soft fur.

Dad nodded sadly. "OK, we'd better go. See you in a couple of days," he said to Abi. He glanced at Mum. "Thanks for inviting us to the carol concert, it was brilliant to hear them sing."

Mum looked at Dad and nodded.

Dad hugged Harry and gave Bo a stroke. Abi was just about to say goodbye when Mum spoke again. "Why don't you come round?" she said. "Sandra as well, of course. There's enough mince pies for everyone."

Dad looked surprised. "Really?" he asked.

"Brill!" Harry grinned.

"Why not?" Mum said. "It is Christmas."

*

"While shepherds washed their socks by night," Dad sang.

"Dad!" Harry and Abi giggled.

Abi looked round at her family and was filled with a warm feeling. Everyone was laughing and singing while Mum played the piano.

Harry nudged Abi and pointed to under the piano stool. Bo and Jazz were curled up together, asleep.

"Sometimes we fight like cats and dogs," Harry grinned. "But sometimes we get on as well as Bo and Jazz!"

Abi giggled, then sighed happily as she looked at her beautiful pets, and her happy family. It wasn't even Christmas Eve yet, but already all her Christmas wishes had come true!

Read on for lots more . . .

🐾🐾🐾🐾

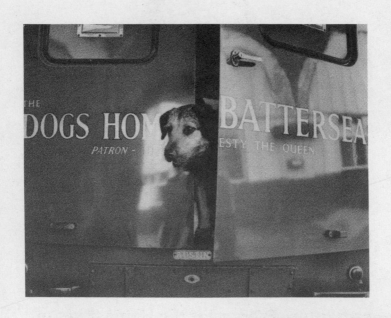

Battersea Dogs &
Cats Home

Battersea Dogs & Cats Home is a charity that aims never to turn away a dog or cat in need of our help. We reunite lost dogs and cats with their owners; when we can't do this, we care for them until new homes can be found for them; and we educate the public about responsible pet ownership. Every year the Home takes in around 9,000 dogs and cats. In addition to the site in southwest London, the Home also has two other centres based at Old Windsor, Berkshire, and Brands Hatch, Kent.

The original site in Holloway

History

The Temporary Home for Lost and Starving Dogs was originally opened in a stable yard in Holloway in 1860 by Mary Tealby after she found a starving puppy in the street. There was no one to look after him, so she took him home. She was so worried about the other dogs wandering the streets that she opened the Temporary Home for Lost and Starving Dogs. The Home was established to help to look after them all and find them new owners.

Sadly Mary Tealby died in 1865, aged sixty-four, and little more is known about her, but her good work was continued. In 1871 the Home moved to its present site in Battersea, and was renamed the Dogs' Home Battersea.

Some important dates for the Home:

1883 – Battersea start taking in cats.

1914 – 100 sledge dogs are housed at the Hackbridge site, in preparation for Ernest Shackleton's second Antarctic expedition.

1956 – Queen Elizabeth II becomes patron of the Home.

2004 – Red the Lurcher's night-time antics become world famous when he is caught on camera regularly escaping from his kennel and liberating his canine chums for midnight feasts.

2007 – The BBC broadcast *Animal Rescue Live* from the Home for three weeks from mid-July to early August.

2012 – Paul O'Grady's hit ITV1 series and Christmas Special, *For the Love of Dogs*, follows the stories of many Battersea dogs.

The process for re-homing a dog or a cat

When a lost dog or cat arrives, Battersea's Lost Dogs & Cats Line works hard to try to find the animal's owners. If, after seven days, they have not been able to reunite them, the search for a new home can begin.

The Home works hard to find caring, permanent new homes for all the lost and unwanted dogs and cats.

Dogs and cats have their own characters and so staff at the Home will spend time getting to know every dog and cat. This helps decide the type of home the dog or cat needs.

There are three stages of the re-homing process at Battersea Dogs & Cats Home. Battersea's re-homing team wants to find you the perfect pet: sometimes this can take a while, so please be patient while we search for your new friend!

1 Register details

2 Match

3 Leaving with your new pet

Have a look at our website: **http://www.battersea.org.uk/dogs/ rehoming/index.html** for more details!

Fingerprint dogs and cats.

Thumb print over corner of scrap paper and remove to leave white triangle for nose and mouth.

Stick-on eyes: Hole-punched pieces of paper with dots marked in the centres.

Or use white paint to make eyes and tummy.

Making a Mask

Copy these faces onto a piece of paper and ask an adult to help you cut them out.

Jokes

WARNING – you might get serious belly-ache
after reading these!

**What do you get when you cross a
dog and a phone?**
A golden receiver!

What is a vampire's favourite dog?
A bloodhound!

**What kind of pets lie around the
house?**
Car-pets!

**What's worse than raining cats and
dogs?**
Hailing elephants!

**What do you call a dog that is a
librarian?**
A hush-puppy!

**What do you get when you cross a
mean dog and a computer?**
A mega-bite!

 **Why couldn't the Dalmatian hide
from his pal?**
Because he was already spotted!

What do you do with a blue Burmese?
Try and cheer it up!

Why did the cat join the Red Cross?
Because she wanted to be a first-aid kit!

What happened to the dog that ate nothing but garlic?
His bark was much worse than his bite!

What do you get if you cross a dog with a Concorde?
A jet-setter!

What do you call a cat that has swallowed a duck?
A duck-filled fatty puss!

Did you hear about the cat that drank five bowls of water?
He set a new lap record!

Did you hear about the cat that swallowed a ball of wool?
She had mittens!

Dos and Don'ts of looking after dogs and cats

Dogs dos and don'ts

DO

- Be gentle and quiet around dogs at all times – treat them as you would like to be treated.
- Have respect for dogs.

DON'T

- Sneak up on a dog – you could scare them.
- Tease a dog – it's not fair.
- Stare at a dog – dogs can find this scary.
- Disturb a dog who is sleeping or eating.

- Assume a dog wants to play with you. Just like you, sometimes they may want to be left alone.
- Approach a dog who is without an owner as you won't know if the dog is friendly or not.

Cats dos and don'ts

DO
- Be gentle and quiet around cats at all times.
- Have respect for cats.
- Let a cat approach you in their own time.

DON'T
- Stare at a cat as they can find this intimidating.

- Tease a cat – it's not fair.
- Disturb a sleeping or eating cat – they may not want attention or to play.
- Assume a cat will always want to play. Like you, sometimes they want to be left alone.

Some fun pet-themed puzzles!

Common Dog Breeds

Here is a list of some common dog breeds. See if you can find them in the word search. The words can be written backwards, diagonally, forwards, up and down, so look carefully and GOOD LUCK!

AMERICAN
BULLDOG
BEAGLE
DOBERMAN
GERMAN
SHEPHERD
GREYHOUND
JACK RUSSELL
AKITA
LABRADOR
LURCHER
MONGREL
ROTTWEILER
HUSKY
BULL TERRIER
SHIH TZU
SHAR PEI
BULLMASTIFF

Can you think of any other breeds? Write them in the spaces below

Tangled Leads and Crazy Maze

Oh dear! The Battersea staff are walking three dogs but the leads are tangled. Can you find out which dog belongs to which person by following the leads?

George

Michelle

Chris

Spikey

Joe

Sammy

Tessa

Start here

Who's walking who?

George is walking _ _ _ _ _ _
Michelle is walking _ _ _ _ _ _
Chris is walking _ _ _ _ _ _

Remember: while in public all dogs must wear a collar and tag and should be kept on a lead.

Remember: always take a poop-scoop bag with you and clean up after your dog.

"Yummy yummy! Three big juicy bones for me." says Tessa, but can you help her find her way through the maze to find the bones?

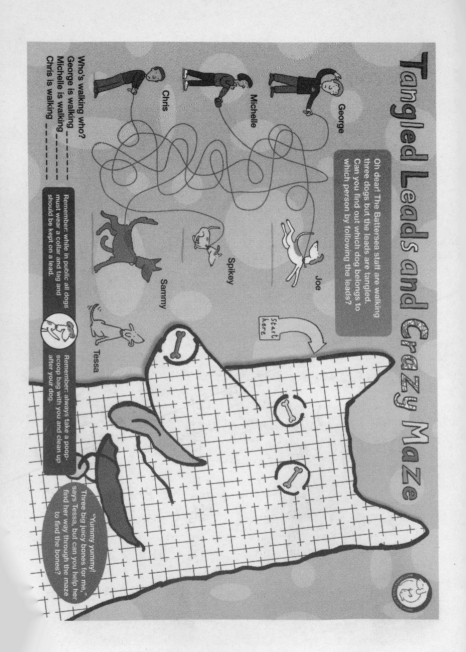

Drawing dogs and cats

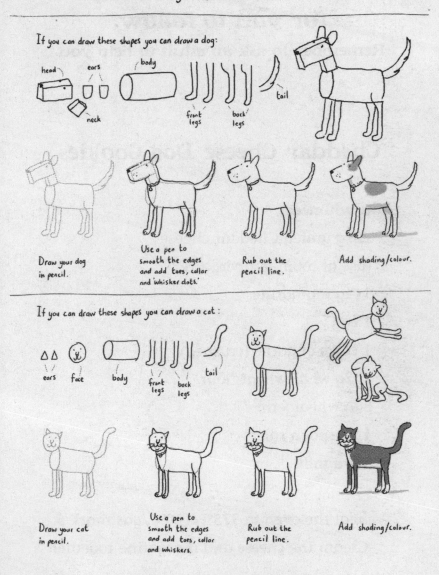

If you can draw these shapes you can draw a dog:

head ears body tail
neck front legs back legs

Draw your dog in pencil.

Use a pen to smooth the edges and add toes, collar and 'whisker dots.'

Rub out the pencil line.

Add shading/colour.

If you can draw these shapes you can draw a cat :

ears face body front legs back legs tail

Draw your cat in pencil.

Use a pen to smooth the edges and add toes, collar and whiskers.

Rub out the pencil line.

Add shading/colour.

Here is a delicious recipe for you to follow:

Remember to ask an adult to help you.

Cheddar Cheese Dog Cookies

You will need:

227g grated Cheddar cheese
(use at room temperature)

114g margarine

1 egg

1 clove of garlic (crushed)

172g wholewheat flour

30g wheatgerm

1 teaspoon salt

30ml milk

Preheat the oven to 375°F/190°C/gas mark 5.

Cream the cheese and margarine together.

When smooth, add the egg and garlic and mix well. Add the flour, wheatgerm and salt. Mix well until a dough forms. Add the milk and mix again.

Chill the mixture in the fridge for one hour.

Roll the dough onto a floured surface until it is about 4cm thick. Use cookie cutters to cut out shapes.

Bake on an ungreased baking tray for 15–18 minutes.

Cool to room temperature and store in an airtight container in the fridge.

There are lots of fun things on the
website, including an online quiz, e-cards,
colouring sheets and recipes for making
dog and cat treats.

www.battersea.org.uk